FROM DONNA
25/12/02.

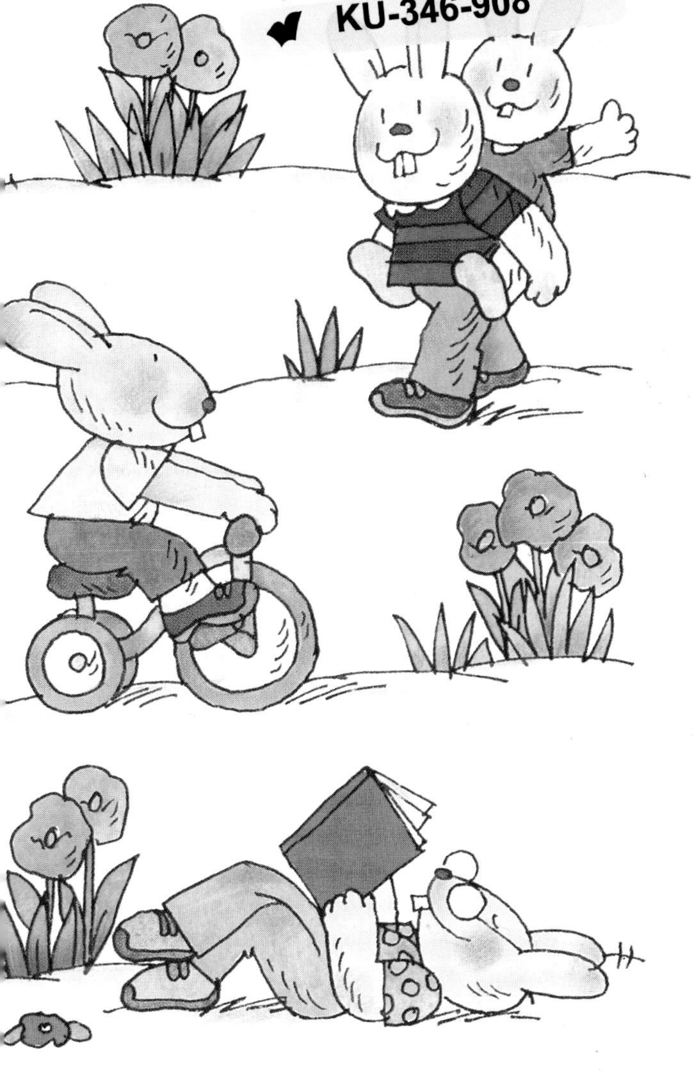

Contents

Sally and Sam go shopping   4

The lost sock   6

By myself   8

Can you touch?   10

I want to drive   12

Brand new tooth   14

Sneezes   16

Disappearing ducks   18

Cake   20

Yes! Yes!   22

Bathtime   24

Hugs   26

British Library Cataloguing in Publication Data
Stimson, Joan
   Storytime for 1 year olds.
   I. Title   II. Astrop, John   III. Astrop, Caroline
823.914[J]
   ISBN 0-7214-1419-2

First edition

Published by Ladybird Books Ltd   Loughborough   Leicestershire   UK
Ladybird Books Inc   Auburn   Maine 04210   USA

Printed in England (3)

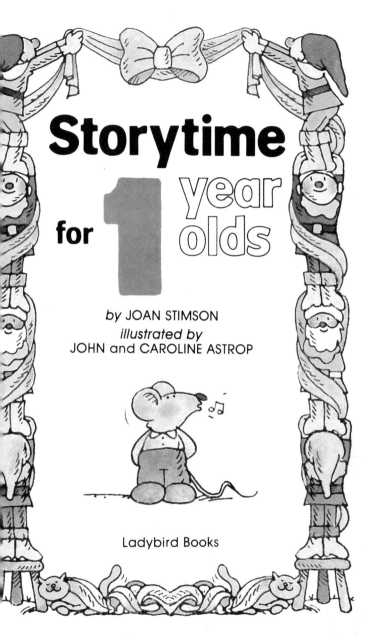

Storytime

for **1** year olds

by JOAN STIMSON

illustrated by
JOHN and CAROLINE ASTROP

Ladybird Books

Sally and Sam go shopping

Sally and Sam are shopping with their Mum.

Mum is pushing a big trolley.

'Don't play with the toilet rolls,' Mum tells Sam. 'They might run away.'

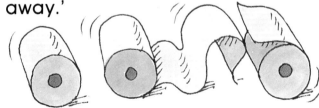

'Don't play with the eggs,' Mum tells Sally. 'They might break.'

When they get home, Mum opens a small paper bag.

'PUFF, PUFF, PUFF!'

Mum blows as hard as she can. She gives a yellow balloon to Sally and a red one to Sam.

'NOW,' says Mum, 'you can play... AS MUCH AS YOU LIKE!'

The lost sock

Lucy has lost one
of her socks.
She can't find it
anywhere.

It isn't in her bedroom.
It isn't in the bathroom.
It isn't in the kitchen.

It isn't in the hall.

'Where IS that
silly old sock?'
Lucy asks Teddy.

'THERE it is!'
she cries.

'It's on YOUR foot. And it's been
there… ALL THE TIME!'

By myself

Ben is at the park with Dad. He climbs up the steps to the slide.

'Catch me!'
cries Ben.

'WHEEEEE!' Ben whizzes down the slide and Dad catches him.

Ben runs over to the swings.

'Lift me up and push me!' cries Ben.

'SWISH, SWOOSH.' Dad pushes Ben backwards and forwards.

The ice cream van comes to the park.

'DING-A-LING!' Dad buys an ice cream for Ben.

'Shall I help you?' asks Dad.

'No, thank you,' says Ben. 'I can eat it ALL... BY MYSELF!'

Can you touch?

Can you touch your tummy?

Can you touch your toes?

Can you touch your eyes and ears?

Now, what about your... NOSE?

I want to drive

I want to
drive a
tractor

I want to drive a train

I want to drive a red, red bus

Then FLY home in a plane

Brand new tooth

Can you see my brand new tooth,
Brand new tooth, brand new tooth?
Can you see my brand new tooth?
It's VERY new and white!

Can you FEEL my brand new tooth,
Brand new tooth, brand new tooth?
Can you FEEL my brand new tooth?
I GREW IT IN THE NIGHT!

Sneezes

Someone needs a tissue

Someone's going to sneeze

ATISHOO! ATISHOO!

Pass a tissue please

Disappearing ducks

Quackety, quackety, quack!
Why DON'T the ducks come back?

Quackety, quackety, HEY!
Why DO they run away?

Cake

This is the cake
Straight out of the tin

This is the cake
With currants in

This is the cake
The very last one

Let's EAT the cake
Look... ALL GONE!

Yes! Yes!

'MOO MOO,' says the cow
As she sits in the sun.

'BAA BAA,'
says the lamb
'I'm having
such fun!'

'WOOF WOOF,' says the dog
As she waits
by the door.

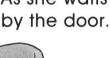

'MEOW MEOW,' says the cat
'I'm washing my paw.'

'COME IN,' calls Dad
As he stands by the sink.

'YES! YES!' cries the girl
'We ALL need a drink!'

Bathtime

If toes were little fishes
And the bath a great big sea
Then TEN little fishes
Would be swimming after...

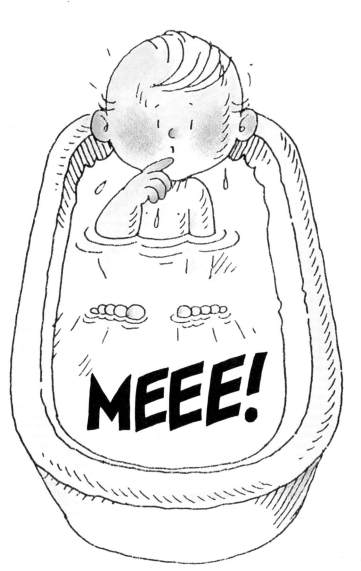

Hugs

Would you like to hug a hippo?

Would you like to
hug a croc?

Would you like to hug an ELEPHANT?
...I think you'd get a shock!

Would you like to
hug a panda?

Would you like to hug a sheep?

Would you like to
hug your
TEDDY BEAR?

...IT'S TIME TO GO TO SLEEP!